Dear Parent:

Congratulations! Your child is taking the first steps on an exciting journey. The destination? Independent reading!

STEP INTO READING® will help your child get there. The program offers five steps to reading success. Each step includes fun stories and colorful art. There are also Step into Reading Sticker Books, Step into Reading Math Readers, Step into Reading Phonics Readers, Step into Reading Write-In Readers, and Step into Reading Phonics Boxed Sets—a complete literacy program with something for every child.

Learning to Read, Step by Step!

Ready to Read   Preschool–Kindergarten
• big type and easy words • rhyme and rhythm • picture clues
For children who know the alphabet and are eager to begin reading.

Reading with Help   Preschool–Grade 1
• basic vocabulary • short sentences • simple stories
For children who recognize familiar words and sound out new words with help.

Reading on Your Own   Grades 1–3
• engaging characters • easy-to-follow plots • popular topics
For children who are ready to read on their own.

Reading Paragraphs   Grades 2–3
• challenging vocabulary • short paragraphs • exciting stories
For newly independent readers who read simple sentences with confidence.

Ready for Chapters   Grades 2–4
• chapters • longer paragraphs • full-color art
For children who want to take the plunge into chapter books but still like colorful pictures.

STEP INTO READING® is designed to give every child a successful reading experience. The grade levels are only guides. Children can progress through the steps at their own speed, developing confidence in their reading, no matter what their grade.

Remember, a lifetime love of reading starts with a single step!

Special thanks to Diane Reichenberger, Cindy Ledermann, Jocelyn Morgan, Kim Culmone, Tanya Mann, Emily Kelly, Sharon Woloszyk, Carla Alford, Rita Lichtwardt, Kathy Berry, Rob Hudnut, David Wiebe, Shelley Dvi-Vardhana, Gabrielle Miles, Rainmaker Entertainment, and Walter P. Martishius.

Visit us on the Web!
StepIntoReading.com
randomhouse.com/kids
www.barbie.com

Educators and librarians, for a variety of teaching tools, visit us at RHTeachersLibrarians.com

ISBN 978-0-449-81628-8 (trade) — ISBN 978-0-449-81629-5 (lib. bdg.)

Printed in the United States of America   10 9 8 7 6 5 4 3 2 1

Random House Children's Books supports the First Amendment and celebrates the right to read.

STEP INTO READING®

STEP 2

Barbie
Mariposa
& the
Fairy Princess

Fairy Dreams

Adapted by Mary Man-Kong

Based on the screenplay by Elise Allen

Illustrated by Ulkutay Design Group

Random House 🏠 New York

Mariposa is a
Butterfly Fairy.

She lives in Flutterfield.

She has many friends.

Mariposa visits
the queen.
"Go to Shimmervale,"
says the queen.
The Crystal Fairies
live there.

The Crystal Fairies think Butterfly Fairies stole magic crystals. The crystals give life to the kingdom.

Mariposa must make peace
with the Crystal Fairies.
She is worried.

Mariposa goes
to Shimmervale.
She meets
King Regellius
and Princess Catania.

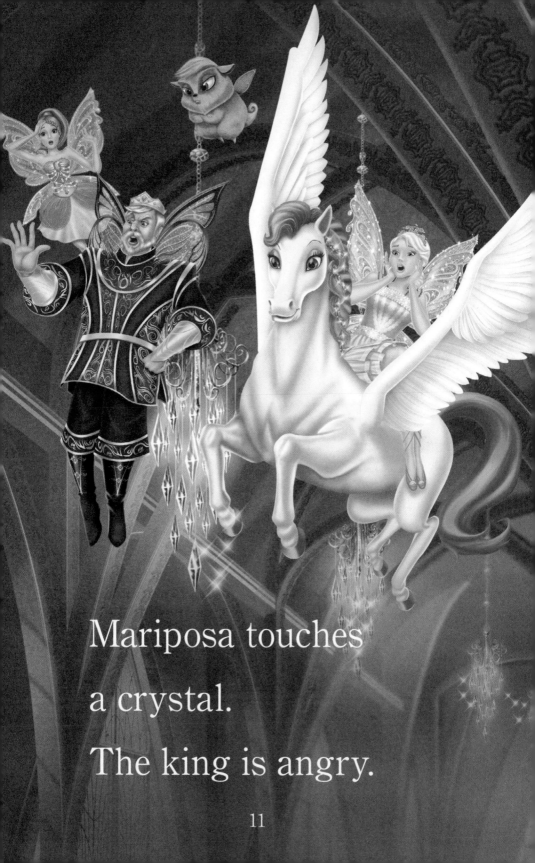

Mariposa touches
a crystal.

The king is angry.

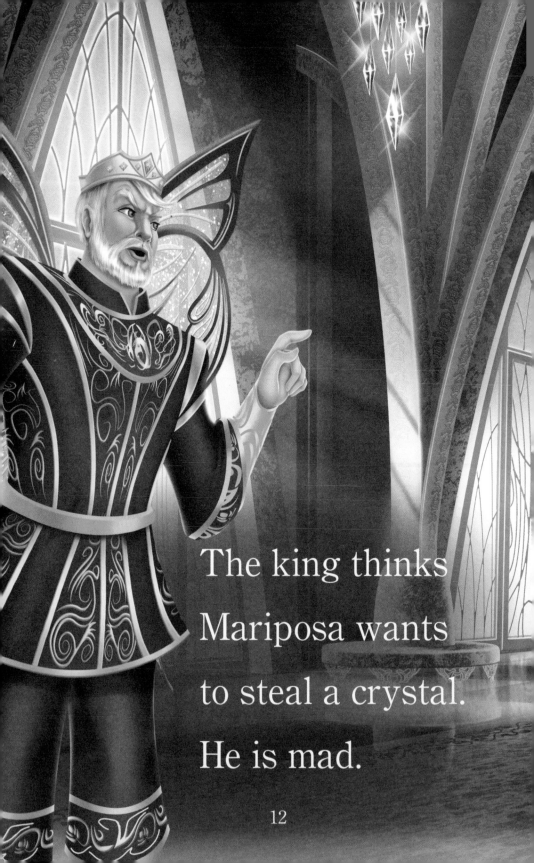

The king thinks
Mariposa wants
to steal a crystal.
He is mad.

Mariposa is sad.
She is not
making peace
with the Crystal Fairies.

Princess Catania
takes Mariposa
to Glow Water Falls.
They laugh.

They skip
rainbow rocks.
They become
good fairy friends.

Catania tells Mariposa
a secret.
She cannot fly.

She goes everywhere
on her flying horse.
Catania dreams of flying.

The princess gives
Mariposa a shiny
crystal necklace.

Mariposa gives
the princess
a magical
Flutter Flower.

Mariposa and Catania
get ready
for the Crystal Ball.
Mariposa's dress
sparkles and shimmers!

Mariposa and
the princess dance.
The fairies have fun!

Mariposa drops
her crystal necklace.
The king thinks
Mariposa has stolen
the crystal!

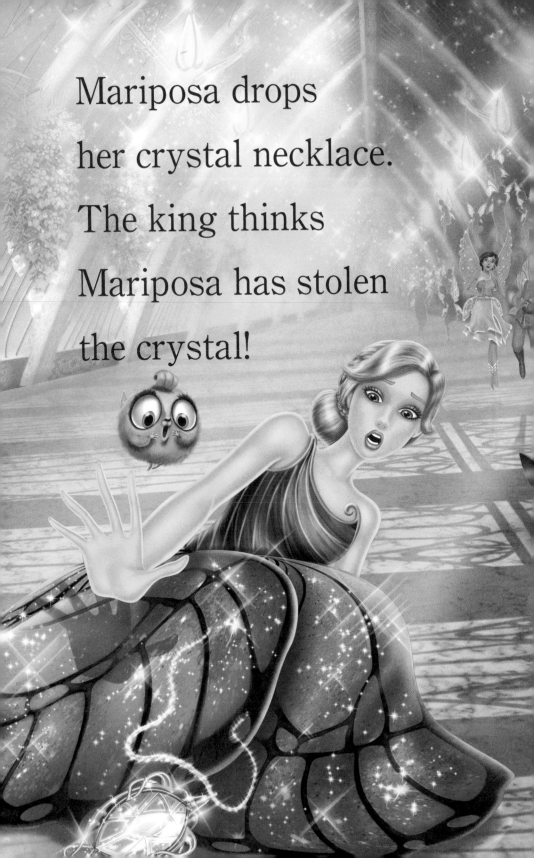

"Leave Shimmervale!"

he orders.

Mariposa is very sad.

Mariposa sees
an evil fairy flying
to Shimmervale.

Mariposa will help
the Crystal Fairies.
She is a good friend.

Mariposa needs
Catania's help.
But Catania is afraid.
She cannot fly.

Mariposa tries
to save the powerful
Heartstone Crystal.
The evil fairy freezes her!

Catania learns to fly.
She defeats
the evil fairy!
But it is too late.
The crystals are under
the evil fairy's spell.
The kingdom
grows weak.

The fairies still have
the Flutter Flower.
They place it near
the Heartstone Crystal.
The crystal glows.
The other crystals
come to life.
The kingdom is saved!

Catania and Mariposa
dance at a fairy party.
They shimmer, flutter,
and fly!
They are best
fairy friends!